First published by Parragon in 2009

Parragon
Queen Street House
4 Queen Street
Bath BA1 1HE, UK

ISBN 978-1-4075-6684-9

Printed in Poland

Bath · New York · Singapore · Hong Kong · Cologne · Delhi · Melbourne

It was morning at the pet shop. Most of the puppies jumped and yipped, hoping to be adopted. But not Bolt. He was playing happily, waiting for his special person to find him. Then, suddenly, there she was! Bolt sat up straight and wagged his tail - which he couldn't resist chasing.

"You're my good boy," the little girl said, hugging him.

There was no doubt about it. They were a team.

Bolt didn't know it then, but he wasn't being adopted into any ordinary family. Penny's father was a professor who had some top-secret scientific information. And a cat-loving green-eyed villain named Dr. Calico wanted that information very badly.

Penny's dad was worried about keeping Penny safe from Dr. Calico. So one night, he took Bolt to his laboratory and gave the pup amazing powers. From then on, it would be Bolt's job to protect Penny.

One day, Dr. Calico captured Penny's father.
Penny knew that she had to rescue her dad. And Bolt knew
that he had to help Penny.

Soon Bolt and Penny were on their way to find Dr. Calico's secret hideout. But Calico's thugs tried to stop them!
Bolt used his amazing powers – speed, agility, heat vision, and his super bark. Soon the thugs were defeated, and Penny was safe.

"Good job, buddy," Penny said, picking up Bolt and carrying him into a trailer with his name on it. Bolt didn't see the bad guys getting up unharmed as the trailer door closed. In fact, He had no idea that his adventures weren't real. He, Penny, Dr. Calico, the professor, and the thugs were actors in a Hollywood TV show!

At the shooting of the next episode, Dr. Calico appeared and captured Penny! Bolt lunged to save her, but he felt something pulling him back. The poor dog couldn't see that it was an animal handler taking him back to his trailer. Filming was done for the day.

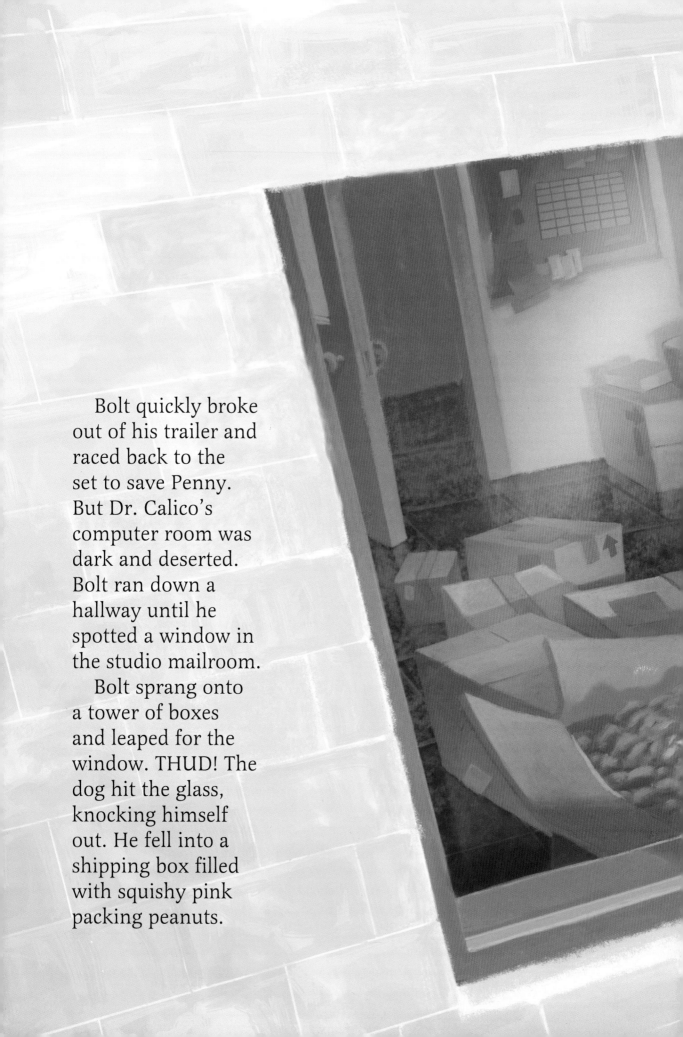

Bolt quickly broke
out of his trailer and
raced back to the
set to save Penny.
But Dr. Calico's
computer room was
dark and deserted.
Bolt ran down a
hallway until he
spotted a window in
the studio mailroom.

Bolt sprang onto
a tower of boxes
and leaped for the
window. THUD! The
dog hit the glass,
knocking himself
out. He fell into a
shipping box filled
with squishy pink
packing peanuts.

The next day, Bolt woke up and broke out of the box. He had been shipped overnight from Hollywood to New York City!

He ran down the strange streets until – SMACK! – he slammed into a fence and got his head stuck. Bolt couldn't bend the bars, so he thought that the pink packing peanuts had taken away his powers. Fortunately, three friendly pigeons helped free him.

Bolt asked the birds how to find Calico. "I need someone on the inside. Someone close to the green-eyed man. A cat!"

"A cat?" said a pigeon named Vinnie, smiling slyly. "We know just the one."

The pigeons flew off, and Bolt followed.

The cat Vinnie had in mind was named Mittens, and she was one tough kitty. She got her meals by threatening pigeons for half of the food they found.

"When my stomach growls, I have no control over these claws!" she warned them.

Suddenly, Bolt burst into the alley and slammed Mittens against a trash can. She was a cat, so she must be an agent of Dr. Calico - and know where Penny was being held prisoner.

"Where is she?" he demanded.

"Would you tell this crazy canine he's got the wrong cat?" Mittens pleaded with Vinnie and his pals.

But the pigeons weren't about to help her - not after the way she had treated them.

Bolt tied Mittens to himself with a leash. He would need her to find Calico – and Penny. Spotting a moving lorry with a Hollywood sign, Bolt tried to use his heat vision on its lock.

"If I stare really hard, it will burst into flames and melt," he explained. But nothing happened. Mittens thought he was crazy. The movers opened the door to the truck, and Bolt and Mittens snuck on board. Mittens accidentally tipped a box over. Bolt panicked when he saw the pink packing peanuts that had weakened him. He threw himself and Mittens out of the lorry.

Just then, Bolt's stomach growled loudly. He smelled food cooking at a nearby campsite! Mittens was hungry, too, so she started coaching him to perfect a cute "dog face." Sure enough, as soon as Bolt began begging, the campers happily gave him their scraps.

After finishing their meal, Bolt and Mittens were surprised by something rolling toward them.

"Oh my gosh, oh my gosh, oh my gosh!" a hamster named Rhino cried. "You're Bolt! You're fully awesome!"

"Wait a minute," Mittens said. "You know this dog?"

Bolt was surprised, too. How did this hamster know him? Rhino must work for Penny's dad, Bolt thought. The dog didn't realize that Rhino had been watching him on TV.

"I've captured this cat," Bolt explained. "She's taking me to Penny."

Rhino was ecstatic. He was going on a mission with his hero! Moments later, the trio was standing on an overpass as a train roared by below them.

"Every time he did this on the magic box it was awesome!" Rhino said to Mittens.

At last, Mittens understood: the "magic box" was a TV. Bolt was an actor! Before she could stop him, Bolt was swinging them all down onto the train.

The three animals landed on top of the train – and fell right off! Amazingly, none of them were hurt. Fearing for her life, Mittens climbed a tree to get away from Bolt.

"Look, genius," Mittens told the deluded dog, "you're not real. Penny's not real. Nothing you think is real, is real."

But Bolt didn't believe her. And unfortunately, their arguing caught the attention of an animal-control officer!

Rhino had rushed off to find a ladder to help Bolt get Mittens out of the tree. But by the time he arrived with the ladder, it was too late. Alone in his little plastic ball, Rhino watched as the animal-shelter van pulled away with Bolt and Mittens locked inside.

Rhino knew what he had to do . . . Destiny was calling. He would answer and rescue Bolt!

Rhino raced after his hero. He climbed out of his
ball and up the side of the van. Then he pulled on the
door handle with all his might. The door flew open –
and Bolt leaped out!

"I did it!" Bolt cried, thinking that he had broken
out with his amazing powers.

"Fully awesome!" Rhino greeted Bolt excitedly.

"You . . . you opened the door?" Bolt asked in
disbelief. That was when Bolt finally realized that he did
not have amazing powers after all. It was the worst moment
in his life. He was no hero. He was just a dog – a heartbroken,
ordinary dog.

But, hero or not, he knew that he had to rescue Mittens. So
Bolt and Rhino headed off to find the animal shelter.

When they reached the shelter, Rhino grew giddy –
he was part of a prison break!

Since Bolt couldn't rely on his powers anymore, he had to
work out another way to free Mittens. Thinking
fast, he sent Rhino rolling into the dog pen. The dogs barked
excitedly, and the animal-control worker went to
investigate. With the coast clear, Bolt sneaked past and
tiptoed into the cat room.

"You came back for me?" The cat asked, surprised.

Rhino caught up with Mittens and Bolt, and the trio headed
for the door. But an animal-control worker blocked the way.

Suddenly, another worker ran up and slipped, accidentally
kicking Rhino's ball into a helium tank. The tank shot off like
a rocket and crashed into the shelter sign outside. The sign
fell onto a lorry carrying a petrol tank, and . . . KA-BOOM it
exploded! Bolt, Rhino, and Mittens ran for their lives.

The three friends jumped into a house that was being moved by a big lorry.

"If I don't fight bad guys, then what am I?" Bolt asked, sad and confused. "What do dogs do?"

"Being a dog is EASY," Mittens reassured him. "You can do almost anything and people will love you."

And so Mittens began teaching Bolt how to be a normal dog. She showed him where dogs like to sleep on a cold night. And she taught him how to drink from a toilet.

"Rhino is awesome!" a voice suddenly echoed through the house. "He's beyond awesome. He's be-awesome!"

Bolt and Mittens followed the sound until they found Rhino yelling into an air vent. He loved the way it made his voice sound loud and powerful. Bolt stepped in front of the vent and enjoyed the air blowing on his face. That gave Mittens an idea . . .

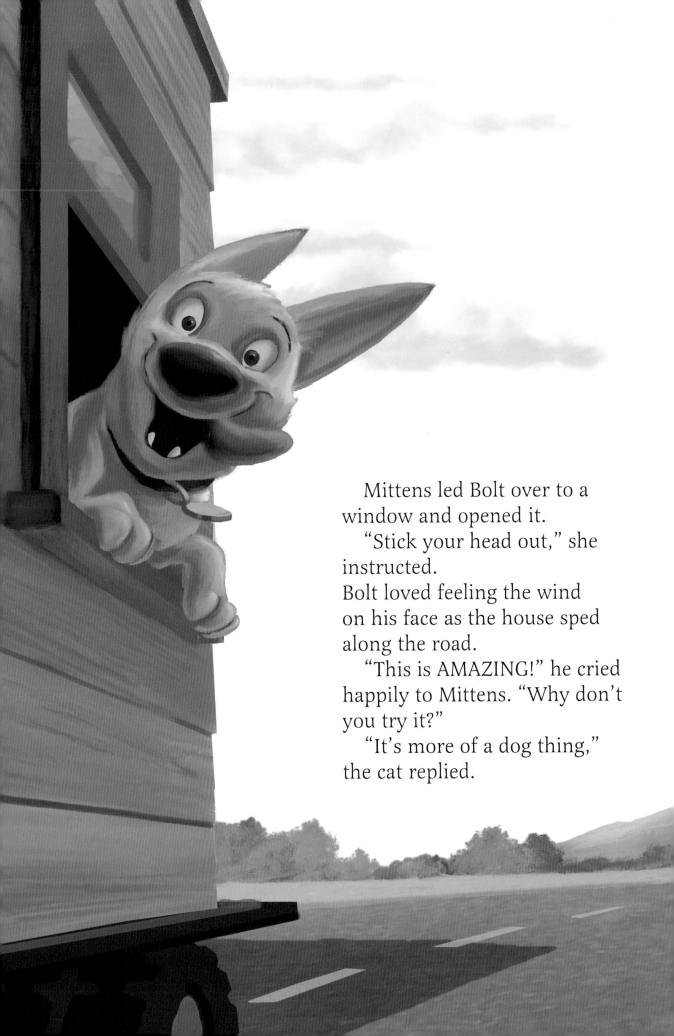

Mittens led Bolt over to a window and opened it.

"Stick your head out," she instructed.
Bolt loved feeling the wind on his face as the house sped along the road.

"This is AMAZING!" he cried happily to Mittens. "Why don't you try it?"

"It's more of a dog thing," the cat replied.

Days passed, and the animals continued their journey across the country. Mittens used the time to teach Bolt to play fetch . . .

bury a bone . . .

and chase a spurting sprinkler.

All the while, Mittens was surprised by how much she was learning to trust and like Bolt. It was almost like having a family.

One rainy day, Mittens, Bolt, and Rhino
were riding in the back of a lorry. Bolt
was happy as could be. The raindrops
washed away the lightning bolt on
Bolt's side, but he hardly
noticed.

Bolt the TV star was gone,
and Bolt the regular dog
had taken his place. Mittens
smiled. She had a new
friend.

Eventually, the animals arrived in Las Vegas. Mittens loved it there so much that she set up homes for the three of them. But Bolt still wanted to find Penny.

"She's from a television show," Mittens argued. "None of it is real!" Long ago, Mittens had her own person, and that person had left her. She didn't want Penny to break Bolt's heart, too.

But Bolt wouldn't give up. He knew that Penny still loved him.

"Every dog needs his person, and she's my person," Bolt insisted. So he set off to find her.

When Mittens told Rhino about Bolt, the hamster freaked.

"If Bolt has taught me anything," Rhino declared, "it's that you never abandon a friend in a time of need."

Rhino rolled off to find his canine friend. Mittens thought for a moment. Then she followed.

Not long after, Bolt finally made it back to Hollywood.
As soon as he arrived on the set, he heard Penny!

"Bolt! Bolt! You're okay!" she shouted. Bolt ran towards the
sound of her voice, overjoyed. He couldn't wait to see her and
play fetch with her! Then he stopped short.

Another dog raced into Penny's arms. Bolt had been
replaced! He slipped away unseen, his heart broken.

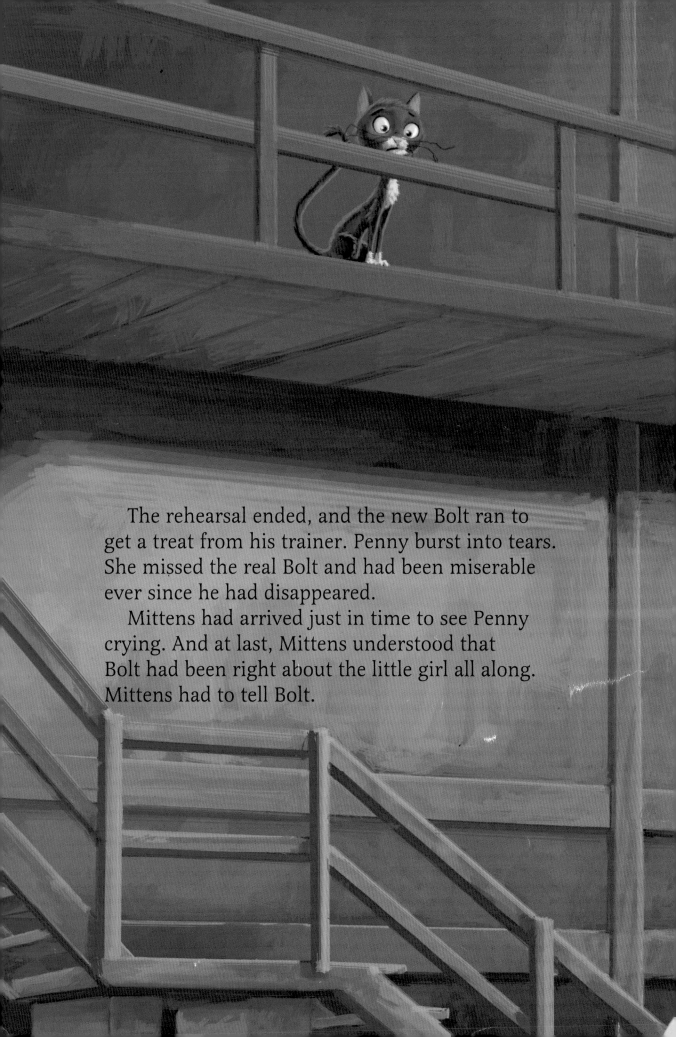

The rehearsal ended, and the new Bolt ran to get a treat from his trainer. Penny burst into tears. She missed the real Bolt and had been miserable ever since he had disappeared.

Mittens had arrived just in time to see Penny crying. And at last, Mittens understood that Bolt had been right about the little girl all along. Mittens had to tell Bolt.

Mittens found Bolt wandering sadly outside the studio.
"What are you doing here?" Bolt asked.

"That's not important," said Mittens. "Listen, I was wrong about Penny. I saw the whole thing! She was devastated. She's your person, Bolt. And you are her dog."

Suddenly, Bolt's ears shot up. He had heard someone cry for help. The TV studio had caught on fire!

"It's Penny!" he shouted.

With no time to lose, Bolt leaped into the burning building as a piece of the set crashed down behind him. Bolt was able to find Penny in the darkness and guide her over to an air vent. But Penny was too weak to go on. She told him to leave and save himself – she loved him that much.

But Bolt would not desert her. He might not be a super-dog, but he was Penny's dog. Bolt barked as loudly as he could. Firefighters heard the barks through the vent and burst into the burning room. Thanks to Bolt, Penny was saved!

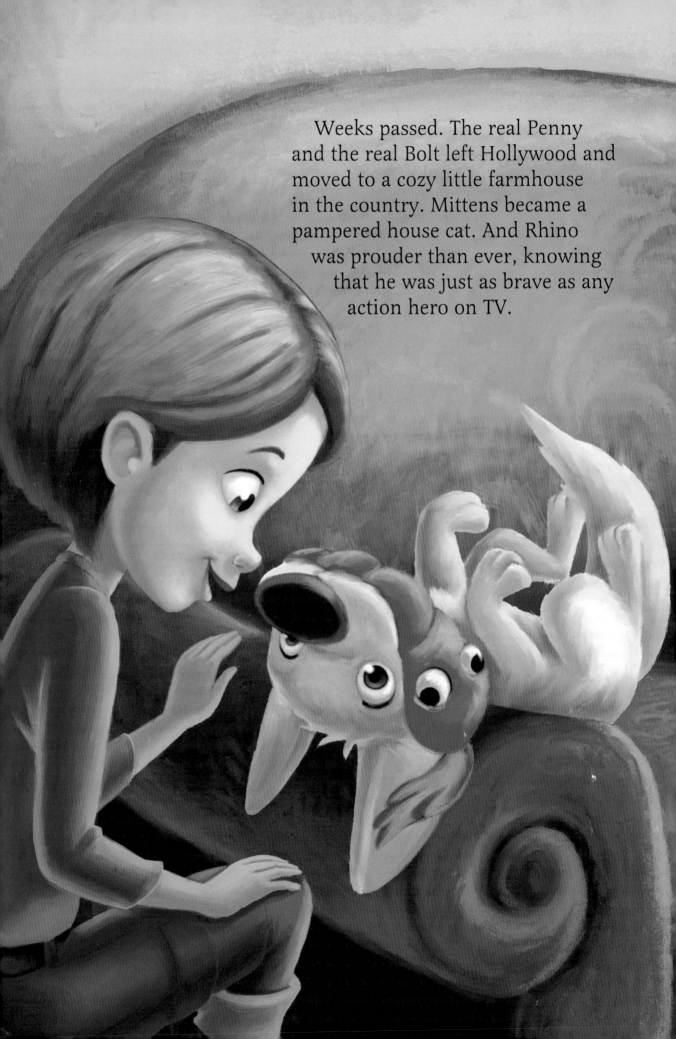

Weeks passed. The real Penny
and the real Bolt left Hollywood and
moved to a cozy little farmhouse
in the country. Mittens became a
pampered house cat. And Rhino
was prouder than ever, knowing
that he was just as brave as any
action hero on TV.

At last, Bolt knew who he really was - a regular dog.
And he had learned an important lesson - that special powers don't make you a special dog. Once you've found your special person, a regular dog's life is just about the most perfect life there is.